Amelia's Book of Notes & Note Passing
(a note notebook)

by Marissa Moss
(except all notably noted
and notated notes by Amelia)

Take note of it!

Simon & Schuster Books for Young Readers

This is a
looong way to
send a note.

New York   London   Toronto   Sydney

A good
place for
bank notes!

When do I get
to pass notes here?

This is
almost a
Torn note, but
not quite.

.|||| 2012   CH

SIMON & SCHUSTER BOOKS FOR YOUNG READERS
An imprint of Simon & Schuster Children's Publishing Division
1230 Avenue of the Americas, New York, New York 10020

Copyright © 2006 by Marissa Moss

SIMON & SCHUSTER BOOKS FOR YOUNG READERS
IS A TRADEMARK OF SIMON & SCHUSTER, INC.

Amelia® and the notebook design are
registered trademarks of Marissa Moss.

Book design by Amelia ← note design by Amelia too!
(with help from Lucy Ruth Cummins)

The text for this book is hand-lettered.
Manufactured in China

2   4   6   8   10   9   7   5   3

CIP data for this book is available
from the Library of Congress.

ISBN-13: 978-0-689-87446-8   ISBN-10: 0-689-87446-4

Amelia's
Book of Notes
&
Note Passing

> CLASS NOTICE
> Please welcome our new
> student, Maxine!

Normally who cares about new students? It's their job to figure out how to fit in, where to go, what to do. All you have to do is be nice so they don't have a horrible first day. I know how it feels to be the new kid — I've done that. So of course I was polite to Maxine. I showed her the right place in the textbook. I smiled. Okay, I didn't give her my extra slide when we were looking at bacteria, but I let her have the good microscope, the one without a crack on the lens.

And she smiled back at me. She seemed nice. But now I'm not sure. All because of the nasty notes.

Writing and reading have been two of my favorite things for as long as I can remember. I've always thought of paper and pens as my friends. Not anymore. Now they're my enemies. Enemies in the form of nasty notes. The question is <u>who</u> made them my enemies. That's where the new girl comes in. The ugly notes all started after she came to our school. Besides, there's something about her I don't trust.

"I hate her!" Carly clenched her fists at her side.

I put my arm around her. "Come on, Carly, you're right — we know what kind of person she really is and she's not worth the paper she wrote on." I kicked the notes at our feet. "And she's not as tough as she looks. For a minute she almost cried."

"I saw that," Leah agreed. "She was almost human — almost. But she still doesn't know how to be a friend. She doesn't have a clue."

I put my other arm around Leah. SHE knew how to be a friend.

You're right. She's a jerk and that puts her down at the bottom of the heap.

Right next to the smelly people and Hallway Lurkers.

Come on — that's the bell. We don't want to sink to Maxine's level and be Hallway Lurkers!

At lunch Carly, Leah, and I sat together. I didn't see Maxine and I didn't care. I was happy — for the first time in days.

"Look what I have in my lunch," Carly said, handing each of us a fortune cookie. "It's time for a good note — a lucky one."

I bit into my cookie and pulled → out the fortune.

You have friends who are loyal and true.

I didn't need a cookie to tell me that, but it's the perfect <u>note</u> to end on.

This notebook is dedicated to

Asa,

a loyal, true friend

who finds interesting notes,

and to Rob,

my best, best friend.

Here's what I know about her.

Maxine is very stylish and careful about her hair, her fingernails, and her clothes. She moved here from Los Angeles, and she's always name-dropping movie stars she _says_ are her friends. Yeah, right. →

She's in 6th grade too, but she looks and acts more like an 8th grader. She says that's because she's "sophisticated", and we're all hicks. At first it seemed like no one was good ← enough to be her friend. Then she zeroed in on the one girl she thought was cool enough to hang around with.

That one girl was...

Carly, my best friend →

She's cool but in a nice way, not in a mean, snotty way. ←

Of course, Maxine would never look at me — I'm beneath her notice, like some kind of crumb on the floor. Except Carly likes me. We sit next to each other when we can. We eat lunch together. And after school we walk home together. And because Carly's so cool, a little bit of her coolness rubs off on me. That's not why I like her — besides being cool, she's smart and funny and sweet. But it's a nice bonus, since there's no way I'd be cool on my own.

Reasons why I'm NOT cool

My mom cuts my hair even though I BEG her not to! Her way of trimming bangs is to put masking tape across my forehead and chop away.

Mom doesn't let me buy clothes that look good and are in style. All she cares about are price — it has to be cheap — and what she calls "wearability", meaning how long something will last. Unfortunately "sturdy" is NOT a nice description when it comes to clothes. And it's even WORSE for shoes.

I'm still not allowed to get my ears pierced. I must be the last girl on the planet with this problem.

So I'm not surprised Maxine didn't try to be friends with me. Why should she? And I'm not surprised she'd want to be friends with Carly. Who wouldn't want that? But I am surprised that once she decided to go after Carly she didn't include me in her plans. Just the opposite.

Carly and I were eating lunch together — as usual — when Maxine came up.

"Hey, Carly," she said. "Can I sit with you?" Not "Hey, Carly, hey, Amelia." Not "Can I sit with you guys?" She was crystal clear about that.

Naturally Carly, being a <u>nice</u> person, was welcoming to the new girl.

"Sure, of course," she said. "So how do you like Ms. Reilly?" Since we're in 6th grade, we change classes each period and science with Ms. Reilly is one of the classes we have together.

Maxine was too busy unpacking her lunch to answer.

← sushi lined up in a beautiful box

↑ cute container of wasabi

↑ adorable container of soy sauce

It was the most elaborate lunch I've ever seen. She took an extra-long time, placing everything just so, like it was a dramatic performance and she wanted to be sure to impress Carly with her amazing, wondrous lunch.

And it worked. Carly was impressed — I could tell. She stopped chewing her sandwich and watched silently as Maxine displayed her edible treasures.

Maxine expertly picked up a sushi roll with the chopsticks.

"Would you like one?" she offered. Not to me, of course, but to Carly.

"Thanks!" Carly reached for it with her fingers. "I love sushi! You're so lucky to get that in your lunch."

My own lunch looked miserable in comparison. What could I possibly tempt Carly with?

cold hot-dog sandwich — bordering on bleecch

orange — ho hum

peanut butter cookies — okay, these are tasty, but ordinary, nothing special

"I just love wasabi, don't you?" Maxine said, an instant expert on exotic, unpronounceable foods. "At my old school we once had a wasabi tasting to see which kind was the best."

That was my first clue that Maxine was a liar. I mean, what school would do that? And why? And do different brands of wasabi even exist here? I didn't know there was such a vast choice in Japanese food, but maybe in Los Angeles where she came from that's true. Still, it seemed highly unlikely.

But Carly believed it. And she was impressed again. "That's so cool! You must miss your old school. We never do stuff like that here."

Maxine sighed dramatically. "Yes, I do miss it. But I'm sure there are great things about this school. You'll have to show them to me."

I was gritting my teeth so hard, my jaw ached. Couldn't Carly tell what a phony Maxine was?

"Sure!" Carly smiled. "Amelia and I would love to do that."

I wiggled my eyebrows furiously, trying to signal to Carly to count me OUT, to count herself out too.

Somehow Carly didn't get my secret eyebrow message. But I'm pretty sure Maxine did. And she didn't like what she saw.

"Amelia!" Maxine turned to me as if she'd just noticed my existence. "Such an original haircut. You really must tell me where you get it done — so I can be sure NOT to go there." She laughed like it was a great joke we all could enjoy — only I didn't see anything funny about it.

But Carly did! She laughed.

Then she put her arm around me — as if THAT made it okay.

You don't want Amelia's mom to cut your hair — she's a butcher with scissors, a real public safety hazard.

I couldn't believe it! My best friend was laughing AT me! I shrugged her arm off.

"C'mon, Amelia, don't be mad," Carly coaxed. "We always laugh about your mom giving you haircuts. You think it's funny too!"

I didn't say anything. I couldn't with Maxine sitting there smiling so smugly. But I was thinking it's one thing laughing at something together with your best friend, and it's another when <u>someone else</u> makes fun of you. Couldn't Carly see that?

Just then the bell rang and lunch was over — saved by the bell! Maxine packed her stuff up quickly, especially considering how long it took her to UNpack it.

"I guess I'll see you tomorrow. I have French now."

Carly leaped up. "So do I! I wonder if we're in the same class."

They were. Off they went, chattering away — in French! And off I stomped to my next class, math, with a horrible pounding headache — not a good way to face 45 minutes of equations.

I tried to focus on the problems in front of me, but all I could think of was Carly. →

I <u>had</u> to talk to her, to convince her of Maxine's phoniness before it was too late. ↙

I could just imagine the two of them laughing at me all through French class.

All I could hear was them making fun of me — I wasn't listening to Mrs. Church at all.

Obviously I didn't know the answer to problem 17, and now I have an extra page of homework to do. I felt like Maxine was putting a curse on me. Then when I got to my locker, I <u>knew</u> she was hexing me. That was when I got the first note.

It looked like an innocent piece of paper, neatly folded into a → triangle.

Someone had slid it through the crack in the locker ↙ door.

Usually mail is an exciting thing. Everyone loves to get cards and letters. Packages are even better. But this note was NOT the good kind of mail. It was ugly. It was mean. It was poisonous. It said:

If this note had a face, it would be covered in warts. →

OMG! Do people still cut their hair that way?! Like there's a bowl over their head? What's WRONG with you that you go out in PUBLIC like that?! GET A CLUE!!

← The second time in ONE day my hair was insulted. I wished I was BALD!

I read it and felt a sour stab in my stomach. I couldn't read it twice. I couldn't even examine it for clues about who wrote it. I had to throw it away as fast as possible.

It was so toxic, it made the whole trash can steam with its putrid stench. →

I threw the orange from my lunch on top of it, trying to sink it. I wanted it far, far away.

Even with the note gone, I was so upset, I was shaking. Who hated me so much they would write such mean words? I couldn't imagine. Then I heard a laugh — two laughs. It was Maxine and Carly walking down the hall. Could Maxine have slipped the note into my locker? When would she have had time? Wouldn't Carly have seen her do it? It didn't seem possible, but who else could it be? After all, she'd made that nasty remark about my haircut. And could it be a coincidence — new girl arrives, new nasty note appears? It had to be Maxine — evil, mean Maxine!

I closed my locker and walked toward them, pretending nothing was wrong.

I was trying so hard to look normal, my face felt stiff. →

Hey, Carly. Hey, Maxine. Sounds like French was a lot of fun.

Carly grinned. "You should have heard Maxine! She asked the teacher what 'les fesses' means, and he got all embarrassed. It was a crack-up! Too bad we don't all have French together."

I nodded. I had Mr. Le Poivre for French too, but not the same period as Carly. "Ha, ha, that's funny," I said, NOT laughing. Omar had asked the same question in my class last week. So "les fesses" meant W — behind, tush, bum. So what? That was hilarious?

a row of fesses on a bench — or lots of w's

"So, Carly," I went on. "You're coming over today after school, right?"

Carly stopped laughing. "Oh, I forgot about that. Maxine invited me to her house." She looked at Maxine as if she was waiting for Maxine to ask me over too.

Maxine looked at a spot above my head. "I'd invite you, Amelia, but my mom said I could only have one person over today."

I turned to follow Maxine's gaze. Since she was talking to the bulletin board behind me, maybe it would answer her. After a few minutes it seemed clear the bulletin board would not cooperate, so I had to say something.

"That's okay," I lied. I faced Carly. "You go without me."

"Okay." Carly didn't look at all upset. "See you later then."

Byeeeee!

↑
Maxine drew out the "eeee" in "Bye" so it sounded like there were two syllables. Just that little thing made her sound very happy to leave me behind. Just that little thing made me miserable.

Maxine looked like she'd gotten her way. A smug, self-satisfied smirk twitched on her face. I wanted to punch that smile right off of her, but all I could do was get my books and head to English.

After school I waited for Carly at our usual place, but she never showed up. I guess she'd gone right home with Maxine. So I walked home alone.

The day was gray and cold, but not as gray and cold as I felt inside. →

It was one of the worst days of my life.

As I passed by houses, all cheery and lit up like whoever lived there was happy, I thought about all the bad things that had happened to me in my entire life. I wondered how today measured up against those other bad days.

Some things are bad but in a small, annoying way, like burnt toast, a pebble in your shoe, a pop quiz. Other things are bad in a BIG way, like Cleo, my awful sister, like the first time I had an asthma attack, like my dad leaving when I was just a baby. I wasn't sure where today fit in, but it seemed pretty bad.

small bad stuff
↓

↑
mosquito bite

cold hot-dog sandwich
↑

sniff, sniff
a stuffy nose
↑

BIG BAD STUFF
↓

I get an evil note —
badness: 10
↓

↑
My sister, Cleo, sits next to me on the bus for the field trip and pukes — badness: 6

Carly abandons me for Maxine — badness: 10
↑

I waited for Carly to call that night, but she never did. A bad day was turning into a bad night. I had horrible dreams.

In one dream Carly and Maxine were best friends and I was completely shut out. I followed them around school, hoping for a chance to join in, but it never happened. I was all alone, a fate worse than death in middle school.

When I woke up, I worried that my dream was coming true. I wanted to wear something so cool that Carly would like me again, but there were two problems with that — one, I didn't _own_ anything cool, and two, Carly had never been the type to care about stuff like that. That's why she was my friend in the first place. And anyway, just because she'd gone over to Maxine's house didn't mean she didn't like me anymore. But if _I_ don't like Maxine, then she can't either or she's breaking one of the rules of best-friendness — the enemy of my friend is MY enemy. I had to remind Carly of that!

So I wore what I normally wear and went to school. Luckily PE was first period and that's a class I have with Carly — WITHOUT Maxine.

When I saw Carly, I tried to act like my usual self.

"Hey," I said.

"Hey," she said.

"How was Maxine's?" I asked.

"Okay," she answered.

I wasn't sure, but something seemed just a little bit off. Was I imagining it or was Carly not as friendly as usual?

"So how about today?" I asked.

"Today what?" Carly looked blank.

"Today after school. You're coming over, right?"

"Um, oh, that." Carly was careful not to look me in the eye. "I don't think that'll work today — maybe later."

Carly didn't say she had plans, but I got the feeling she definitely did. Only not with me — with Maxine.

Then it was time for basketball and we couldn't talk much, but that was okay because by the end of the period, we were our old selves again, joking and laughing.

I'm terrible at sports, especially basketball, where being short (like me) really matters, but it was fun anyway to run around the court, to practice dribbling and free shots. As our muscles loosened up, so did we, and I knew Carly was my best friend again.

I wanted that feeling to last all day, but what would happen when we went to science? What would happen when Maxine was around?

Lucky for me, Maxine was late to class, so Carly and I sat next to each other. While the teacher was taking attendance, Carly passed me a note.

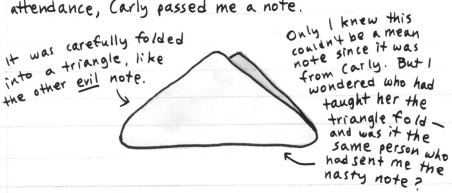

It was carefully folded into a triangle, like the other _evil_ note.

Only I knew this couldn't be a mean note since it was from Carly. But I wondered who had taught her the triangle fold — and was it the same person who had sent me the nasty note?

I quietly unfolded the note on my lap under the desk, so the teacher couldn't tell what I was doing. But even though I could see it, I couldn't read the note — it was a jumble of letters, nonsense words.

```
UIJT  JT  JO  DPEF.  IFSF  JT
UIF  LFZ.  XSJUF  UIF  BMQIBCFU
JO  B  DJSDMF.  HP  POF  MFUUFS
UP  UIF  SJHIU  PG  UIF  MFUUFS
ZPV  XBOU  BOE  VTF  UIBU
OFJHICPS  MFUUFS  JOTUFBE.
USZ  JU  BOE  TFF  IPX  FBTZ
JU  JT  UP  VTF!
        D B S M Z
```

Carly looked over at me to see if I had figured it out. I shook my head. Was this Maxine's code? Something _she_ invented? I looked at Maxine, but she was busy finding her homework to hand in. She wasn't paying attention to me or Carly. I stared at the note again, trying to make sense of it. The last five letters, DBSMZ, were trying to tell me something. Then I remembered that's how Carly used to sign her name — I had it! I knew the code! I tried my idea and it worked. This is what the note translated to:

THIS IS IN CODE. HERE IS THE KEY. WRITE THE ALPHABET IN A CIRCLE. GO ONE LETTER TO THE RIGHT OF THE LETTER YOU WANT AND USE THAT NEIGHBOR LETTER INSTEAD. TRY IT AND SEE HOW EASY IT IS TO USE!   CARLY

Carly was grinning at me — she could tell I'd solved it. →

I smiled back. Of course she was still my friend! No way Maxine could steal her away!

I wanted to send a note back to her right away. But I had to be discreet. If Ms. Reilly catches you passing notes, it means DETENTION — I didn't want that.

Good thing I can write sorta neatly without even looking at the paper. I did the best I could, folded my note into a tiny rectangle, and kicked it on the floor toward Carly's foot. Here's what I wrote:

J MPWF ZPVS DPEF. J IBWF BO JEFB IPX
UP NBLF JU FWFO USJDLJFS. PO FBDI EBZ XF
TLJQ POF NPSF MFUUFS TP VIF DPEF
DIBOHFT. USZ VIJT TFOUFODF:
AQW HKIWTGF KV QWV!
COGNKC

What I really wanted to say was how glad I was to have her for a friend, but that seemed a little mushy for a note. Anyway, I didn't need to say it. I was smiling so much, I was sure Carly could tell what I was thinking.

Carly was looking at me, waiting for a chance to pick up the note, when Maxine accidentally on purpose dropped her pencil. It rolled right next to the note! Maxine got up and bent over to pick up the pencil — and the note, too. Except Carly was quicker and she stepped on it before Maxine could grab it. She almost stepped on Maxine's fingers!

I glared at Maxine. She knew that note wasn't for her! What was she, anyway, some kind of mail thief? The rest of class took forever — the slowest 20 minutes of my life. Finally the bell rang, and Carly snatched up the note before she gathered up her stuff.

I waited for her in the hall. Only when she came out, Maxine was with her!

Why did you try to grab Carly's note? That wasn't for you!

How was I supposed to know that? I didn't see her name on it or anything.

↑ I was furious!

she was infuriatingly calm! ↗

"It was just a simple misunderstanding," Carly said. "No harm done. And Maxine apologized to me."

"Well, she didn't apologize to _me_!" I said. I was FURIOUS at Carly, too How could she stand up for Maxine? That was breaking another rule of best-friendness.

"Oh, Amelia, I'm so, _so_ soooorry." Maxine drawled, making it perfectly clear she wasn't sorry at all.

"See — that's that!" Carly grabbed my arm and pulled me down the hall. "Let's go eat lunch!"

Maxine slipped her arm around Carly's other arm. "Yes, let's."

I wanted to talk to Carly and remind her how friends are SUPPOSED to act. I wanted to talk with her IN PRIVATE. Most of all, I wanted Carly to be my friend again, not some evil traitor. Instead I was stuck with Maxine eating her fabulous lunch of Chinese chicken salad.

I concentrated on chewing my fish-stick sandwich (another of Mom's gross lunch specialties) until Maxine got up to throw away her trash. I only had a minute, but I used it as best I could.

What's up with you and Maxine? I need to talk to you — WITHOUT her around.

Sure, no problem. I'll walk home with you, okay?

I was <u>so</u> relieved. Carly was still my friend. She hadn't gone over to the dark side after all. But then Maxine came back, sat down next to Carly, and whispered something in her ear.

Carly laughed. I frowned. I mean, how RUDE! I tried to act like I didn't care.

How nice — a little humor for dessert is so pleasant.

Perhaps you could share the cause for your merriment; allow the laughter to spread.

I don't think I fooled anyone.

"Hah!" Maxine barked. "Could you say that again in plain English? You must be speaking some strange kind of dialect."

"Really?" I arched an eyebrow. "I'm sure Carly understood me. Didn't you, Carly?"

Carly looked embarrassed. She knew just how obnoxious Maxine was being. I waited for her to stick up for me. I waited a loooooong minute. Then the bell rang and it was time for class. Lucky for Carly because she didn't have to say anything. Lucky for me because I didn't have to see Carly NOT stand by me. Maybe she would have. Now I'd never know.

"See you after school," I said.

"Yeah." Carly nodded. She still looked embarrassed.

"Ta-ta!" Maxine said, wiggling her fingers. I couldn't help it. Just her voice, just the way she moved her fingers — I HATED HER!

I couldn't make a voodoo doll of Maxine, so I did the next best thing. I drew one. When I get home, I can stick it with real pins, but for now I can label what curses will happen when that part of the body is poked. It was very satisfying.

Real voodoo dolls are shapeless → lumps.

My paper one was much more realistic.

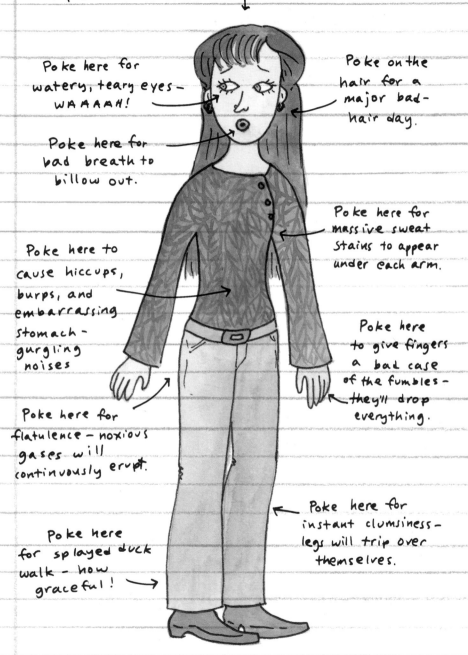

Just drawing the voodoo doll made me feel MUCH better. Then I got to my locker and felt MUCH worse. There was another note in it — even nastier than the first one.

It was SO foul, I could barely stand to touch it. I threw it away as fast as I could.

Amelia—
Take a bath! You're polluting the whole cafeteria. Even Sloppy Joes can't cover your stink!

I took deep breaths trying to calm myself. Who could hate me that much? It **had** to be Maxine. I hated her, so she must hate me. But to be **that** vicious? I would never say those things to anyone, no matter how much I detested them. Could it really be Maxine? I didn't know what to think. I had to see Carly. I had to tell her about the notes. She'd know what to do. She always did.

I was relieved to see her waiting for me after school.

I was afraid she'd change her mind and go home with Maxine again, but there she was, trustworthy as ever. And NO Maxine in sight.

Except something felt a little bit off. I couldn't say exactly what. Carly looked the same. She acted the same. She sounded the same. Only she didn't. I began to wonder if she was a Carly clone, a copy substituting for the real thing.

I waited to see what would happen. She brought up Maxine first.

"Um, sorry about that thing back at lunch," Carly said, studying the sidewalk. At last — she apologized. The rules of best-friendness still held. Or did they? Something was <u>still</u> off.

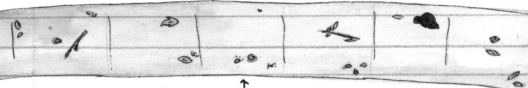

It's amazing how fascinating the ground can be when you want to avoid looking at someone. All I saw were pebbles, twigs, a leaf or two, dog poop to be avoided, but Carly kept her eyes glued to the sidewalk as if the mystery of the universe was written there.

I was going to say something, to ask what was going on with Maxine, to tell Carly about the mean notes, when I noticed something on the sidewalk. All I could tell was that it was a piece of crumpled-up binder paper, but it seemed like a message from the universe. I picked it up and smoothed it out. It could have been a page of homework or part of a report. But it wasn't. It was a note.

2: Alexa

Look, u need to drop it. Vanessa
is making you do this. Look, Alexa,
u were nice and this one girl made
u change. I suggest u leave her
because she is bad for you. She
just wants u to be hurt. If u
don't change, I'm never speaking
to u.

Jasmine

I read it out loud to Carly. The note was so true, it
was creepy! Only I should have written it, not Jasmine. And
it should be to Carly, not Alexa. And instead of Vanessa,
it should say Maxine.

I stared at Carly. "I think this note's for you."

She laughed nervously. "Come on, Amelia, you just found
that on the ground. It's to some girl named Alexa who
probably dropped it on purpose because it was none of
Jasmine's business."

"Are you saying it's none of my business?" I asked.

"Amelia! I'm talking about the note. What are you talking about?"

"You," I said. "And Maxine. She's the one who's bad for you. And you're the one who's changed."

"What do you mean? You're just mad because of the whispering at lunch. Okay, I admit that was rude, but bad manners doesn't make someone evil. It was a mistake, that's all." Carly still wasn't looking at me. Now she was looking up at the power lines.

"Don't you wonder who throws shoes up there and why they do it?" she asked.

"Don't change the subject!" I snapped.

"Come on, Amelia, this is the kind of thing we talk about. It's why I like you so much — you notice stuff like that. It's true I like Maxine, but I'll always like you, too."

I sighed. Carly still liked me. But was she my best friend? Could she be my best friend and still like Maxine? I shook my head. It didn't work that way. She couldn't like both me and Maxine. The universe would implode.

"I'm not wondering about shoes right now," I said. "I'm wondering about notes. Mean notes."

Carly looked at me — finally. "You mean the note Maxine tried to take?"

"That was mean of _her_. But the note wasn't mean."

She was looking at _me_, not up or down, so I told her about the mean notes stuck in my locker.

"Maybe they weren't meant for you," Carly said. "Like the note you just found on the sidewalk."

"What? The notes had my name on them!"

Carly shrugged. "Maybe they got the wrong Amelia's locker."

I shook my head. "So you don't think Maxine did it?"

Carly looked shocked. "Maxine! Why her? Of course not!"

I didn't know why her, but who else could it be? Can people hate you for no good reason?

Just then a piece of paper fluttered by.

It looked like another note. Suddenly I was seeing notes everywhere.

I grabbed it and read it out loud.

Thanks for parking so close! Next time leave a can opener so I can get my car out. Jerks like you should take the bus!

Carly laughed. "Well, that's a nasty note and it's clearly _not_ meant for you. Or me," she added.

"No!" I laughed too. "Though it sounds like something Cleo would write once she starts driving — and parking."

Carly looped her arm through mine. "Listen, the only notes meant for you are the ones I send you, and we have our own secret code so no one else can understand them."

It was like the good old days walking with Carly. We didn't talk about Maxine at all and I liked it that way.

We talked about our code and ways to make it trickier. I was thinking about all the different kinds of notes there are in the world — the kinds left on cars, on doors, in lockers, on refrigerators, in books, the kind you pass in school, and the kind you bring to school after you've been out sick. And the kind you find on the sidewalk, lost notes finding a new home with someone else, taking on a new meaning like some sort of message from the universe.

Once I started looking, I saw notes everywhere! It seemed like people lost notes constantly. Maybe the ones I found in my locker really were a mistake. Maybe they were simply lost notes.

When Carly saw I was picking up scraps of paper to see if there was anything interesting, she started doing it too. Together we found:

a paper doll ↓

a school photo ↓

a ticket stub ↓

Admit One

a shopping list →
I'm sure this was an old person's list. Who else buys this stuff?

baloney
string
horseradish
prunes
buttermilk
light bulbs
butter pecan
ice cream

a playing card ↓

a note →

ARI—
I COULDN'T WAIT ANY LONGER. HAD TO GO. CALL ME.
MIKE

Suddenly I had it! → 💡 The perfect revenge ← flashed in my head!

I told them my idea, and they loved it. Carly couldn't wait to get started, so we decided to be ready for action tomorrow. I almost felt sorry for Maxine — okay, not really, I didn't feel sorry for her at all. I was just eager to see her face once our plan was done.

I would love to wipe that smug smirk off her face. →

And replace it with a sad, droopy mouth. ←

Carly met me after school, just like old times.

"I'm sorry, Amelia," she said. "I never should have listened to Maxine. I shouldn't have let her get to me."

"Yeah!" I agreed. "You shouldn't have!" I smiled at her. "But it's okay. At least you admit when you make terrible mistakes."

Carly shook her head. "I thought I was a better judge of character, but I guess Maxine fooled me because she looked so perfect."

"I know," I said. "She has to look that good to cover up how awful she is or no one would go near her. Talk about two faces! She has a zillion of them!"

"She wrote that I was a two-faced fake! Me, two-faced!" Carly shuddered.

"Talk about two-faced!" I said and put my arm around her. It was horrible that Maxine was mean to me, but I knew she didn't like me. And I didn't like her. It was way worse for Carly. The nasty note she got was more than mean — it was a betrayal, a so-called friend turning into a definite enemy.

I wanted to do something to make Carly feel better. So I said something I didn't really believe.

"Maybe it's not Maxine. We don't have proof she wrote those notes."

"Oh yes, we do!" Leah was adamant. I saw her stick a piece of paper into a locker. What could she be doing? Returning notes she borrowed or delivering her own?"

Leah was all fired up. There was no stopping → her now.

We should teach her a lesson! We should write the meanest, ugliest, nastiest note of all and stick it in HER locker— see how SHE likes getting that kind of note!

Carly shook her head. "No. If we do that, we're as bad as her. And that's something I NEVER want to be."

I liked Leah's idea, but I agreed with Carly, too. There must be a way to give Maxine a taste of her own medicine without stooping to her low level.

My stomach twisted. I was right — it was Maxine who sent me the nasty notes!

"Did she send one to you?" I asked. As bad as I felt, I was relieved I wasn't the only person Maxine hated.

"We've all gotten them." Leah turned to the two girls sitting on her other side. "It's kind of a club now — the nasty note club, courtesy of Maxine."

"I guess I'm a member too, then." I sighed.

"And I'm a member," said a familiar voice. I turned around — and there was Carly!

"She sent YOU one of those ugly notes!" I was shocked. "But she likes you!"

"That's what I thought too, but I guess not." Carly shrugged. "I suppose I was useful to her for a while. Until she got what she really wanted — a boyfriend."

Carly slumped down next to me.

she looked sad and exhausted.

I really thought she was my friend. Now I know she only wanted to be with me so she could get closer to my brothers — gross! When they weren't interested, she dropped me FAST! I feel like a tissue she used to blow her nose on, then wadded up and threw away.

I was relieved that when I got closer, Leah called out to me to come over.

Hey, Amelia! Sit with us!

I forgot how nice Leah could be. Since we didn't have any classes together this year, I didn't see much of her.

"Would you look at that Maxine!" Leah said. "It's disgusting how she throws herself at that boy. Doesn't she have any pride?"

"You know Maxine?" I asked.

"Unfortunately." Leah scrunched up her face like she'd smelled something rotten. "I have English, social studies, and math with her — way too many classes. She's a stuck-up snob in all of them. All she cares about is impressing boys."

"Really?" That was a side of Maxine I hadn't seen. She was too busy trying to impress Carly around me. "I didn't know about that, and she's in my science class."

Leah laughed. "That's a good place for her. — who needs to build a Frankenstein monster when you have her? She's a scientific marvel, the heartless creature from the Black Lagoon."

"A monster? Because she likes boys?" That seemed harsh to me.

"No, because she's mean! Haven't you seen the vicious notes she writes? They're AWFUL! Talk about a poison pen!"

FRIENDSHIP METER

← At the top — best, best friend: someone you talk to every day and can tell all your secrets.

← close friend: someone you spend a lot of time with, but days can go by without seeing each other.

← friend: someone you like, but don't go out of your way to be with. If they're around, fine. If not, that's fine too. Not close enough to trust with a secret.

← acquaintance: someone you don't like or dislike since you don't know them well enough to have an opinion. They're okay either way and someday might move up to friend status (or drop down to enemy).

← familiar face: you've seen this person before, maybe in class, maybe in the hall, but you don't know their name or anything about them except that they sometimes inhabit the same space as you.

← invisible: anyone in a lower grade.

← irritant: someone who bugs you, but not in a big way, more of a minor nuisance.

← enemy: someone you don't like and make sure that they know it.

← deadly enemy: someone you absolutely cannot stand. Even hearing their voice makes your skin crawl. If they're your partner on a project; WATCH OUT!

Anyway, if Carly wasn't with Maxine, I could finally talk to her. If I could find her.

I stood there searching for her, but I didn't see Carly anywhere. The cafeteria was crowded with kids, but I felt so alone. It was worse than being abandoned in a vast desert.

↙

If I stayed there → any longer, I'd get a reputation for being a total pathetic loser. I didn't want to become a cafeteria lurker — I had to sit some where.

I saw a place next to Leah and decided to grab it. She was still a friend even though she wasn't a close friend. At least she was several notches above an acquaintance and WAAAY better than someone whose face you recognize but you don't even know their name.

"Amelia," Ms. Reilly began. "You're a good student, so I didn't expect this from you. Normally, passing notes merits a detention, but I'll excuse you this once. This once," she repeated.

"It'll never happen again," I promised.

"I'm relieved to hear that." She handed me my note. "Here's your property back. Be more careful with your belongings in the future."

One good thing about Ms. Reilly taking my note was I was so worried about that, I forgot to be worried about Carly. Now I could put all my worrying back on her. I needed to talk with her, whether she'd had enough time or not.

I ran to the cafeteria to look for her. I hoped she'd be in our regular spot, waiting for me. She wasn't. I didn't see her anywhere, but I saw Maxine.

Maxine was sitting next to some boy, trying to impress him with her oh-so-elegant lunch. Do boys care about stuff like that? I thought all boys cared about was how a girl looks. I didn't like Maxine, but I had to admit she was pretty — in a bland baked potato sort of way.

"Amelia, I think you know that writing notes in class is NOT allowed. It's not okay to write pass, or read them."

"You should be focusing on science, NOT your social life. That's for lunch and recess."

"Don't read it, don't read it, don't read it," I chanted to myself. If she did, Carly would probably hate me forever for embarrassing her in front of the whole class. "Please, please, please," I begged in my head. If she didn't read it, I wondered if I'd get detention instead. For once I was rooting for detention. I'd rather have a year of that than lose Carly.

Lucky for me Ms. Reilly has a short attention span for anything that's NOT science. She forgot about my note and went on with the lab we were doing.

Which falls faster? How does streamlining speed things up? →

What I really wanted to know was how to make Carly move faster, how to hurry up her decision to get rid of Maxine. But I sure couldn't risk another note! →

Ms. Reilly didn't say anything to me until the bell rang. Then she called me to her desk. I slunk up, waiting to be punished.

She ignored me and Leah, of course, twirled open the lock, and pulled open the locker. The notes tumbled out, a paper snowfall at her feet. I held my breath. Would she ignore them? Kick them away? Read them? Carly and I exchanged nervous looks. Leah bit her li

"Humpf!" Maxine snorted. Then she bent down and picked up a strip of paper. As she read, her lips twitched into a frown. She crumpled up the paper and threw it down, whirling around to face us.

"Did you guys do this?" she accused. "Think you're so smart - you're NO

"What?" asked Carly. "You don't like getting your own notes? Now you know how it feels." She put her hands on her hips, defiant.

Maxine's lips trembled. For a second I thought she was going to cry. Then she snorted. "You are sooooo lame!" She grabbed her books and slammed the locker shut. "I don't care about your stupid notes. You just don't get it, do you?"

"No!" I snapped. "YOU don't get it!"

Maxine ignored me and looked straight at Carly.

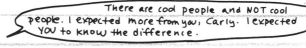

There are cool people and NOT cool people. I expected more from you, Carly. I expected YOU to know the difference.

"I do know the difference!" Carly's eyes flashed. "And I know just what group YOU belong to!"

Maxine rolled her eyes. "Whatever!" She stalked off, leaving an eddy of notes behind.

I woke up excited to put our plan into action. I wanted to look perfect for once, so I snuck into Cleo's room and borrowed a shirt (she buys her own clothes with babysitting money and has MUCH better taste than Mom). I couldn't do anything about my hair or shoes yet, but it was a good start.

Carly grinned when she saw me. "Good going, girl! Nice shirt!"

I twirled around. "Compliments of Cleo!"

"Nice!" Leah agreed. "Now come on, before Maxine gets here."

We all headed for Maxine's locker. The hall was empty except for us. We couldn't help it — we cracked up as we slid the notes in.

I had to admit they were incredibly mean notes. I had to admit that we wrote them. But they weren't OUR words — they were Maxine's. Each of us had made copies of the nasty notes she'd sent us (since we'd all thrown away the originals). And I had to admit it felt GREAT shoving Maxine's ugliness back at her.

Now all we had to do was wait. It didn't take long. As she passed by, Maxine flicked her hair over her shoulder, barely nodding to Carly.

When I got home with Carly, there was a note for me —
a postcard from Nadia!

Dear Amelia,
  Sorry to hear about the
new girl who's so mean. There's
a new girl in my class too, only
she's supernice. She's too nice
to pass any notes, good or bad.
Instead she taps her foot in
Morse code, but I can never
figure out what she's trying
to say. Oh well! At least with
words, you know what's going on.
(P.S. Remember when Twyla
tried to turn me against you? It didn't work!)

Yours till the note pads,
Nadia

Amelia
428 N. Homerest
Oopa, Oregon
97881

I'd forgotten about Twyla, but now that Nadia reminded me,
I could see her clearly — a tall, gangly girl who smelled like
sweet noodle pudding. She was always boasting about how
many friends she had because really she didn't have any. When
she tried to convince Nadia I wasn't worth having as a friend,
the plan backfired, and Nadia hated her for being a lying
creep. And, of course, she stayed my friend. Now it looked like
the same thing was happening with Maxine. It was ~~weird~~
~~weird weird weird~~ weird!
                      ↖ This word just won't behave. It
                         never looks like it's spelled right.

It made me wonder — is there something about ME that makes me an easy target for ugly comments? Is it my bad haircut? My lumpy clothes? My boring shoes? I had to ask Carly. Some things ONLY friends can tell you.

Carly, tell me the truth — are you embarrassed to be my friend?

Am I too uncool for you? After all, Maxine's comments would not have stuck if there wasn't some truth in them.

Carly thought for a while. I held my breath.

Well, there's SOME truth, you're right, but she WAY exaggerated things. I'm not proud of being willing to listen to her, but you know how important being cool is. Still, even MORE important than that is having a friend like you. I don't really care how badly you dress — it just gives me plenty of ideas of what to get you for your birthday.

Then she hugged me and we both felt MUCH better. "Now we have work to do!" Carly said, smiling. "We'll show that girl the power of the pen — let's get writing."

When we finished, we called Leah to check in with her. She was all set too. Tomorrow we'd meet at Maxine's locker before school.

Carly helped me start a scrapbook with the notes we found. Then I added the one she'd passed to me in class and a key that I made so it would be easier to solve our code.

← Carly said she got the idea for this code from her dad. He had a decoder ring like this when he was a kid. Only there were two alphabets, one around the other, so you could dial the ring to solve the code.

P Q R S T U V W X Y Z A B C D E F G H I J K L M N O

← With the letters in an oval like this, it's easier to see which letter you need to go to when you're skipping a space.

It was good to have a project. It helped wash out the bad taste of Maxine and the nasty notes. But then something happened that brought it all back, uglier than ever.

Carly noticed a shirt on my bed.

"Ugh, Amelia, you still have this old thing? Isn't it time to throw it away or give it to Goodwill?"

"Why?" I asked. "I just wore it the other day."

"I know!" Carly groaned. "That's why you need to get rid of it. Maxine said..."

Just these two words — "Maxine said" — they were like a kick in the stomach.

"Maxine said WHAT?!" I yelled. "I knew she hated me! And you don't stick up for me! That's what friends do, remember? That's why you can't like her!"

"She does not!" Carly looked mad, but I felt madder. "She simply said, she said..." Carly sighed, then plowed on. "She said you look like a dork in this shirt. It's so '70s."

"Isn't that a good thing? Aren't the '70s in again?" I asked.

"No!" snapped Carly. "It's a bad thing. The '70s are a decade that should be erased in terms of style. Maxine's right — you have no sense of fashion."

I screamed, "MAXINE!! Who cares what SHE says?! I've ALWAYS dressed like this — I've worn this shirt a million times. And you've never cared before. You're supposed to stick up for me, to tell Maxine to SHOVE it! That's what best friends DO! Now you're sticking up for MAXINE!!!"

I screeched so loudly, my throat felt ragged. Carly looked at me coldly.

"I think I'd better go," she said. "I should have gone to Maxine's house. She doesn't shriek at me."

I wadded up the dork shirt and flung it at Carly. "Go, then! And give this shirt to Maxine when you see her."

Carly stepped over the shirt like it was a pool of poison. She didn't look back. She didn't say good-bye. By the time I went to bed, she still hadn't called to apologize.

It was our worst fight ever.

Part of me felt satisfied because yes, Maxine _was_ as bad as I suspected, telling Carly mean things about me. But most of me was miserable because Carly actually believed the horrible things. I was so upset, I couldn't sleep. Finally I got up and wrote a story. That calmed me down so I could fall asleep.

The Nasty Notes

One day a girl found a nasty note on her pillow.

> YOU HAVE TERRIBLE BREATH! HAVEN'T YOU EVER HEARD OF BRUSHING YOUR TEETH!?

Of course, the girl _did_ brush her teeth and she knew the note wasn't true. Still, it hurt that someone could even think she didn't practice good oral hygiene. She actually began to doubt whether she'd brushed her teeth that morning and hurried to brush again.

The harder the girl brushed, the more the note bothered her. →

And the more the note bothered her, the harder she brushed. ↙

The girl's teeth were sparkling, but the next day there was another note.

> YOUR BREATH SMELLS LIKE YOU CHEW FISH-EYE GUM! DO SOMETHING OR I'LL REPORT YOU AS A FRESH AIR HAZARD TO THE ENVIRONMENTAL PROTECTION AGENCY! NOW!!

The girl felt horrible. After school she rushed off to buy mouthwash and mints. But no matter how much she gargled or how many mints she sucked, the note still made her feel terrible.

The next day she found a third note slipped under her bedroom door. It said:

> I CAN'T STAND IT ANYMORE! STOP BREATHING THROUGH YOUR MOUTH — YOU'RE POLLUTING THE WHOLE WORLD!

The girl felt so awful, she crumpled on the floor and started to cry. "But I __do__ breathe out my nose!" she sobbed. "And my breath isn't bad — at least not worse than anyone else's. Why is someone being so mean to me?"

Her brother heard her crying and came into her room to see what was wrong. She showed him the notes.

"Did you write these?" she asked. "Is this some kind of prank?"

The boy shook his head. "I didn't write them, but I think I know who did. Wait here." He went into his room and came back with a wooden box.

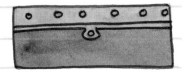

He unlatched the lid and carefully opened it.

Huddled in a corner was a small furry creature with sharp claws and fangs.

All around it were pieces of paper with words scrawled on them.

The girl reached into the box and snatched up one of the pieces of paper. It said: "I KNOW WHO FARTED IN CLASS TODAY! CAN'T YOU CONTROL YOURSELF?!"

"What is this?" she asked, dropping the paper quickly.

"I'm not sure," admitted her brother. "I found it in the attic and it demanded paper and pencils. When I opened the box to check on it, it had written all these mean notes."

"I guess it can escape the box," the boy continued. "It must have left those notes for you to find. I don't know why it's like that."

"Then why don't you get rid of it?" the girl asked.

The boy slammed the lid shut. "It's cool! No one else has one! I want to keep it. Okay, it's mean, but only with words."

"That's the <u>worst</u> kind of meanness," said the girl. "But fine, you keep it. At least now I can ignore the notes."

But the next day there was no new note. Nor the day after that. Finally the girl asked her brother what happened to his creature — was it okay?

"I got rid of it," said the boy. "I took it to school and let it out in the soccer field."

"Why? I thought you liked it." The girl was surprised.

"I did," the boy said, "until it started hiding nasty notes for me."

CAN'T YOU SEE THE GROSS GREEN FILM ON YOUR TEETH? EVERYONE ELSE CAN! DO SOMETHING ABOUT IT OR I'LL CALL THE UGLY POLICE!!

The girl laughed and gave her brother a hug. And neither of them got a nasty note again.

But the other kids in school had some unpleasant surprises.

Hee, hee!

Hee, hee!

The End

In the morning I felt better until it was time for science. I couldn't face seeing Carly and Maxine together, even though I'd been careful to wear something I knew Carly would approve of.

She'd given me this shirt for my birthday last year, so it <u>had</u> to be okay. →

← I hoped one cool shirt could make up for a bad haircut and bad shoes.

I got to class as late as I could without getting marked tardy. I didn't want any awkward time sitting next to Carly and NOT talking to each other. I slipped into my seat and tried not to look at her, but I couldn't help it — I saw Carly and Maxine exchange a glance that said "Ignore her!"

That was fine with me because I was ignoring <u>them</u> first. At least I did until Maxine kicked a note over to Carly. Too bad it ended up closer to my chair than to Carly's.

I almost stomped my foot over the note, but I didn't. I couldn't be a Maxine. Instead I stared straight ahead while Carly picked up the note and read it. I could feel the searing heat of Maxine glaring at me, but I didn't look at her. I just kept my eyes on the blackboard and read the same sentence about kinetic energy 36 times.

When the bell rang, Carly and Maxine got up together without one glance at me. At the door I thought Carly was going to turn around and wave to me. I thought she was going to rush over and apologize and promise never to talk to Maxine again. She didn't. She just flicked a paper into the trash and left.

I wanted to stick out my tongue and say "Nyah, nyah, who wants you anyway?" But I'm in the 6th grade now. I can't act like a baby, even though sometimes it's VERY tempting.

I waited until I was sure they had left — and so had everyone else, even Ms. Reilly. Then I went over to the trash can and looked for the paper Carly had dropped.

I couldn't believe it — it was the note and it was in code, our code! Carly must have told Maxine how to solve it. She'd shared our secrets! I tried to calm myself down so I could read what it said, but I was so upset over Carly's betrayal, I almost didn't care what the note said. The note being in code already told me devastating news — Carly was treating Maxine like a best friend, her new best friend.

OHWV HDW OXQFK EHKLQG WKH JBP. L ZDQW WR PDNH VXUH DPHOLD GRHVQW ILQG XV. HDWLQJ ZLWK KHU ZRXOG VSRLO PB DSSHWLWH!

I tried skipping one letter, but that didn't work. Skipping two didn't work either, and I began to worry that maybe they had their own code, one I didn't know at all. Then I tried skipping three letters, and finally the note made sense: "Let's eat lunch behind the gym. I want to make sure Amelia doesn't find us. Eating with her will spoil my appetite!"

My stomach pitched — I felt queasy and clammy like when I had the flu. What should I do? Confront them? Avoid them?

Maybe the best thing to do was to eat lunch by myself wherever I wanted to go. If they were there, fine. If not, that was okay too. I wasn't eager to talk to the two of them anyway.

On the way to the cafeteria I found three notes. I wished they were for me, but they weren't. The only notes I got these days were bad ones.

Dee—
Did u see how M. looked at me?! I _know_ he likes me!!! ♡ ♡ ♡ ♡ ♡ 4EVER!
K.

Cheryl,
hey, wassup? Wanna head downtown today after school?

Yes, it is SO true! I know becuz he told me himself. This is NO rumor!

I sat by myself and ate my leftover cold spaghetti (Mom's bad lunch ideas strike again!). Now I not only had icky food, I had no one to eat it with, making it taste even _worse_. It's dangerous to eat by yourself in middle school. You need to belong _somewhere_.

Perils of Lunch Alone

Sitting by yourself labels you a Loser, so no one comes to sit next to you, so you look like a Loser, so....

Any food thrown in a food fight ALWAYS finds its way to those poor kids doomed to eat by themselves— SPLAT!

Bullies looking for a victim to pick on naturally zero in on defenseless solitary eaters. With no friends to shield them, they are complete sitting ducks, adding insult to injury (and injury to insult).

Besides the social trauma, there's no one to trade your apple with, no one to share their candy bar with you, no one to feel sorry for the miserable lunch your mom packed so they give you some of theirs. You're food doomed to eat only from home — bleecch!

QUACK!

There's an unspoken ranking of everyone, and once you sink to the bottom of the pile, it's almost impossible to raise yourself up. Where would I fit without Carly?

On the top
↓

Really cool people who do the knowing and don't need to be known by anyone.

Cool people who are known by the really cool people.

↑
With Carly, I'm almost here.

The mass of other people — some nice, some bad, some boring, some interesting, but not cool, though they can have cool friends (really this is below the two cool groups on the side).

↑
Without Carly, I'm here.

Cool people who are nice and know other cool people, which adds to their coolness.

Library people — people with no friends, so they hang out in the library to feel safe.

Hallway lurkers — need I say more?

Jocks — people who play soccer or basketball at lunch.

Smelly people — no one likes them or can even stand to be near them.

Jerks — people no one likes.

Gamers and nerds — people who only like each other and are NOT cool in any way, shape, or form.

Total losers — worse even than smelly people.

I wondered what group Carly and Maxine belonged in — one for snarky, mean people and traitorous friends? I didn't see them anywhere. But I did find another note.

Don't forget to return
library book!!!

Maybe it was a sign that I should go to the library — though I didn't want to become a lonely library person. Maybe it was a sign that I had no idea what to do to get Carly back and was desperate enough to listen to random notes. Maybe it was both. Anyway, I _was_ desperate enough to try anything. So I went to the library.

And there was Carly! With no Maxine in sight! I hadn't thought about what I should say, but I couldn't miss the opportunity.

"Listen, I'm sorry about yesterday," I said, rushing up to her. "I just felt bad that it seemed like you were picking Maxine over me. I knew you wouldn't do that." I wanted us to be friends again. I wanted Carly to write notes to _me_, in our own secret code that no one else knew. I wanted Maxine to move back to her old house and old school and leave us alone.

I waited for Carly to say something, to be her old self again.

"Maybe I am," she said after a horribly long silence.

"Maybe you are what?" I asked.

"Maybe I _am_ choosing Maxine over you. You're the one who forced me to decide. I thought you could _both_ be my friends. I guess I was wrong."

"But we can!" I squeaked, terrified. "I'm not making you pick — it's Maxine. She's the one telling awful lies about me!"

"Well, look who's here. She must have sniffed you out, Carly." Maxine walked up. She must have been in the bathroom. Too bad she didn't have diarrhea and would have to spend the rest of lunch there. "Has Amelia tracked you down for some more of her famous insults?"

"I didn't track anyone down." I tried not to yell, to keep my voice calm. "And I'm NOT insulting Carly."

"Oh? You're insulting me instead?" Maxine shrugged. "Figures."

My face felt hot and red. "I did not!" I sputtered.

"Forget it, Amelia," Carly said softly. She scooped her books up into her backpack. "Gotta go."

I watched them walk out of the library together. I felt as brittle as glass, ready to shatter.

When I'd collected myself and could move again, I headed to my locker. I thought about Carly's last words. She hadn't sounded angry, just sad. Maybe we could still be friends. We'd fought before and made up. That's what friends do. But we'd never had such a horrible fight and there'd never been someone like Maxine involved before. I didn't know what to think — or what to do.

It didn't seem like the day could get any worse. Yet amazingly enough, it did. Another vicious note was waiting in my locker.

It was like a ticking → time bomb...

Can you get any more pathetic? Where do you get your clothes anyway, Goodwill? _Bad_ will?

... made of paper and highly explosive ← words.

I didn't want to read it, but I couldn't stop myself. I crumpled up the paper with trembling hands and threw it away before I could read it again. I didn't want the ugly words to sink in.

The evil creature from my story had struck again ! →

Hee, hee, hee!

And that wasn't the end of the day — I still had English to face — my worst class with my worst teacher, the dreaded Mr. Lambaste. If he was mean to me on today of all days, I'd melt into a puddle on the floor. I was used to him being a jerk — and normally as soon as I set foot into his class, I wore mental armor, a shield to ward off his sharp words. Today I was too fragile to muster up my usual toughness.

← I looked like this...

...but felt like this.

I was wearing clothes, but I still felt like I was naked, like a baby bird before it grows feathers to protect its tender skin.

Luckily Mr. L. ignored me, so I didn't have to ward off any nasty comments or mean remarks. In fact, he didn't insult anyone today, he was too excited about the Shakespeare play we were starting to read, Othello. At first I was too busy feeling sorry for myself to pay much attention to what Mr. L. was saying. But when he described the story, especially the part about Iago, I got really interested. For a play that was written 5 centuries ago, it sounded eerily like my life! In the play, Othello, a black officer in the Venetian navy, is married to Desdemona, a white woman. They're very much in love until Iago, who is Othello's righthand man, decides to ruin his commander.

Iago is intensely jealous of Othello and wants to destroy him, so he starts a vicious rumor that Desdemona is unfaithful. He whispers mean hints to Othello, poisoning his ear with ugly lies. And Othello believes him, putting more faith in Iago's nasty words than in honest Desdemona. Othello is driven into such a jealous rage, he ends up killing the woman he loves. It's a very sad story. And very powerful because it shows that words <u>can</u> hurt — they can even kill.

Of course, Carly wouldn't hurt a fly. But Maxine is a snake like Iago, hissing nasty things into Carly's ear, trying to convince her I'm not a good friend. And it's working!

At least in the play Othello <u>does</u> learn that Iago has been lying all along, only it's too late. Desdemona is dead. That's it — the only solution is to prove to Carly that Maxine's an evil liar!

Except she's more evil than a liar. I <u>do</u> have a bad hair cut. I <u>do</u> wear lame clothes. But I'm still a good person and Carly always saw that before. I needed to show Carly how <u>mean</u> Maxine is. If only I had proof that she's the one leaving me the nasty notes.

HELP!

How could I trap her? I needed a giant, sticky web.

Possible Locker Alarms and Traps

Paint Marker

Smell Catcher

Paint is detonated from spray can when paper is slipped into locker, marking person who did it so all can see.

Small dog lives in locker — when note is pushed in, dog catches scent of hand doing the pushing. When dog is let out of locker, he follows his nose to track down the culprit (unless cafeteria odors distract him).

Siren Alarm

Glue Grabber

Alarm is triggered by paper touching locker — loud noise and flashing lights stun note writer into submission.

Area in front of locker is covered with a special glue that is activated ONLY when slits in locker door are touched (like by a note going through them). When that happens, the glue becomes SUPERSTICKY, forcing culprit to leave shoes behind in order to escape.

Naturally Carly didn't walk home with me, but I called her as soon as I could.

Carly, let me explain something.

Amelia, please, don't bother. I think we need a break from each other, maybe a week, while we both sort things out.

A week?! Why so long? And what are we sorting out? You're my best friend, and I'm sorry I hurt your feelings. But I have to warn you not to trust Maxine.

Funny, she says the same thing about you. Who am I supposed to believe?

Me! I wanted to yell - believe me! But it was too late. Carly had already hung up. She just needs more time, I told myself. Tomorrow she'll be her old self again, and it will be like this past week never even happened. At least that's what I hoped (along with Maxine falling into a ditch and never being seen again).

A week seemed like a looong time. There was only one thing to do — write to Nadia, my best friend before I moved away. Even far away, we were still close and whenever I didn't know what to do about something, she helped me see my choices more clearly. It might take a while to hear back from her since Mom says it's too expensive to call, but I felt better just writing to her.

Dear Nadia,
 HELP! There's a new girl at school and she's saying mean things about me to my friend, Carly, because she wants to have Carly all to herself. The worst part is, Carly actually listens to the new girl and that changes how she sees me, how she feels about me. Short of poisoning this creepy new kid, WHAT CAN I DO? *Yours till the heart beats,* Amelia

Nadia Kurz
61 South St.
Barton, CA
91010

Maybe I could write nasty notes about Maxine and leave them where Carly would find them. After all, since she was saying ugly stuff about me, I should return the favor.

Hmmm...what should I write? I wasn't sure if I would actually <u>do</u> anything with my mean notes, but it felt good making them. Even if no one else ever saw them, putting the words on paper got some of the Maxine poison out of my system.

Maxine still wets the bed — she sleeps in a diaper!

WAAH! WAAH!

Maxine picks her nose and eats it!

Yum! what a delicacy!

Ask Maxine about the time she almost set the chemistry lab on fire.

Oops!

Writing the notes reminded me of the time we went on vacation and my sister, Cleo, and I thought it would be funny to leave notes in the dresser drawers at the hotel we stayed in.

We wrote things like:
↓

Didn't your mother teach you to fold your underwear?

No dirty, smelly socks here, please!

In case of fire, remove all flammable pajamas first.

This is MY drawer — you can use the OTHER drawer.

We got the idea from the toilet, which was wrapped in a big note of its own.

Sanitized for your prote

↑
Don't you feel safe knowing your toilet is carefully wrapped? All my life, notes have been good things — funny or important or informative. Now I know they can be bad, too. I just had to make them work for me, not against me.

I decided to write a note after all — to Carly, not to Maxine. I started to put it in code, but it seemed too important to risk it not being solved right.

This is what I wrote: ↓

Carly —
I'm writing you a note because this whole problem started with notes and maybe that's how it can end. I'm afraid that Maxine says mean things about me that make you not like me. It's like she's pouring poison in your ear — not to hurt y<u>ou</u>, but to poison how you feel about me, to make you not want to be my friend anymore. So I'll admit right now that yes, I'm not as cool as you. I have a bad haircut and wear stupid clothes, but that didn't used to matter to you. You liked the way I saw things, my sense of humor. Who else can talk to you about why shoes are hung on telephone wires? Who else wonders why number threes are jolly and fives are bossy?
I miss you, Carly. I want to be your friend 4ever.

amelia

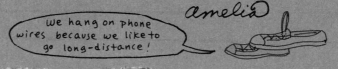

we hang on phone wires because we like to go long-distance!

I slipped the note into Carly's locker before school started. I was so nervous waiting for her to read it, I couldn't focus at all in math. The numbers ran all over the place on my worksheet and I couldn't get them to behave at all.

Then it was time for science, my first class with Carly. I got there before she did and sat down, pretending to read. I didn't have to see or hear her to know when she came into the classroom. The air felt different as soon as she stepped in. I wanted to jump up and hug her, but I kept my eyes glued to the page, holding my breath, waiting to see what would happen.

Since I wasn't looking at her, I couldn't tell if she even glanced at me on the way to her desk. I heard the rustle of her backpack as she passed by and had a clear view of her shoes, but that was it. Except when I looked up, I noticed a small square of neatly-folded paper on the corner of my desk. A note! Carly had left me a note! I grabbed it and stuck it in my pocket. I couldn't follow Ms. Reilly at all as she explained something about earthquakes. I felt like I had an earthquake in my pocket — a seismic shift in my friendship with Carly. I hoped it was a good kind of jolt, a push back together again instead of a widening of the rift between us.

I snuck peeks at Carly the whole period, but I couldn't tell what she was thinking. All I could see was that she wasn't looking at me and that seemed a bad sign.

When the bell rang, she bolted out of her seat without glancing at me — or Maxine. I didn't try to follow her. I needed to read her note first. Then I'd know what to do.

I almost said something to Maxine on my way out, but I didn't. She was studying her fingernails, trying hard to avoid noticing me. It seemed cruel to remind her of my existence.

I found a quiet corner outside the cafeteria (well, as quiet as it can get with clanking trays, clattering silverware, yelling kids, and tromping feet only a hallway away). I took out Carly's note.

Unfolding and reading it seemed better than any fancy-wrapped present. opening

But even though I was excited to have the note, I was also scared. What if Carly was telling me off? What if she hated me now? A mean note from Carly? That would be more than I could stand. The ones from Maxine or whoever it was suddenly didn't seem so bad. At least they weren't from anyone who mattered to me.

As long as I didn't read the note, I could believe Carly was still my friend. I rubbed the paper between my fingers.

I wanted to feel whether the words inside were angry or apologetic, sweet or sour. But I couldn't tell. And as long as I didn't read it, I also didn't know if she'd forgiven me. I couldn't take it any longer — for better or worse, I had to know.

Amelia,
   I have to admit you're right about Maxine. She does say mean things about you, but the way she does it, I'm not even sure it's nasty becuz she acts so concerned — like "Poor Amelia! It must be awful to go around school in those horrible dork shoes!" See, she doesn't say you're a dork, just that your shoes are. Okay, this is a long way of saying that she did make me see you differently. But I don't judge people by how they dress. Just give me some time to figure out this
                                                      Maxine thing.

Phew! SHE DIDN'T HATE ME! But what did Carly mean, she needed time to "figure out this Maxine thing"? Clearly Maxine was a vicious friend thief, trying to steal Carly. How could she not see that? Or was she still deciding whether Maxine was worthwhile as a friend, even if she was a bad-mouthing friend?

   That made me think. You can be friends with a person even when there are things about them you don't like. But there's a limit.

GOOD FRIENDS

someone who gets your jokes — this is way more important than you might think

Someone who's honest with you and tells you stuff that isn't always easy to hear

someone you can do stuff with who likes the same things you do

someone who supports you, no matter how crazy your ideas are

I wish I could show Carly my good friend/bad friend drawings. She would laugh — we would laugh together. This is going to be a very long year if she decides she doesn't want to be my friend anymore.

It was hard, but I didn't call Carly that night. She asked for time, so I was giving her time. But I stared at the phone, willing her to call me. Every now and then, I checked the dial tone to make sure the phone still worked. It did. But no one called.

I slept badly that night. In my dreams Maxine was cutting my hair, making me look really horrible. Carly saw me and screamed. She ran away before I could say anything. Then I looked in the mirror and I screamed too. That's when I woke up, with the snip-snip sound of my ears. Maxine's scissors still in

I tried to pick something cool to wear to school, but when it comes to clothes, I really am like a color-blind clown. I just don't get what makes something hot and something else NOT. Sometimes it seems like a fine line between the two. And sometimes what was cool yesterday is suddenly way UNcool today.

COOL

↑
lip gloss — especially flavored ones, like mango or papaya

↑
flip flops — no matter how chilly it is, these are always in fashion — in fact, the colder, the better

↑
tight, tight T-shirts — buy one size too small, then shrink in the wash for extra snugness

DORKY
↑
medicated lip balm — the smell alone is enough to scream DORKY!

overalls — NEVER in style unless you're a toddler or a farmer →

extraordinary large, shapeless sweaters — they look like you're trying to hide something — yourself! ↘

I thought I looked okay, but I was nervous walking into science class. Carly was already there. She was too busy talking to Maxine to notice me. That was a bad sign. I couldn't hear what she was saying – she was practically whispering – but she didn't look happy. That was a good sign. Maybe they were having a fight. Maybe Carly was telling Maxine she never wanted to see her again. I could only hope.

All during class I kept trying to catch Carly's eye, but she wouldn't look at me. I wondered if I should write another note or if that would be bugging her, not giving her the time she asked for.

Not doing anything was horrible. Even if I didn't give her the note, I _had_ to write it, to do _something_. I tore a corner out of my notepad and started to write.

Carly –
   I want to give you time like you asked, but it's HARD to wait. I need

That was as far as I got when a hand reached down and snatched up the note. I looked up, furious. And suddenly I wasn't angry at all – I was terrified. It was Ms. Reilly! I held my breath. Would she read the note out loud? I know that's what some teachers do when they catch kids passing notes.